Jeremy Strong

Pirate School

Just a bit of wind

Illustrated by Ian Cunliffe

PUFFIN BOOKS

PUFFIN BOOKS

Published by the Penguin Group
Penguin Books Ltd, 80 Strand, London WC2R 0RL, England
Penguin Putnam Inc., 375 Hudson Street, New York, New York 10014, USA
Penguin Books Australia Ltd, 250 Camberwell Road, Camberwell, Victoria 3124, Australia
Penguin Books Canada Ltd, 10 Alcorn Avenue, Toronto, Ontario, Canada M4V 3B2
Penguin Books India (P) Ltd, 11 Community Centre, Panchsheel Park, New Delhi – 110 017, India
Penguin Books (NZ) Ltd, Cnr Rosedale and Airborne Roads, Albany, Auckland, New Zealand
Penguin Books (South Africa) (Pty) Ltd, 24 Sturdee Avenue, Rosebank 2196, South Africa

Penguin Books Ltd, Registered Offices: 80 Strand, London WC2R 0RL, England

www.penguin.com

First published 2002
1 3 5 7 9 10 8 6 4 2

Text copyright © Jeremy Strong, 2002
Illustrations copyright © Ian Cunliffe, 2002
All rights reserved

Printed in Hong Kong by Midas Printing Ltd

British Library Cataloguing in Publication Data
A CIP catalogue record for this book is available from the British Library

ISBN 0–141–31269–6

Contents

1. Pirate Granny

Patagonia Clatterbottom had a big, warty nose and hairs on her chin. She wore a flaming orange wig.

Her arms were as thick as pythons. She had one fat leg and one wooden leg. Her hands were like fat, jumping spiders. In fact she was a pretty scary person. Patagonia Clatterbottom was the head teacher of Pirate School. Every pirate sent their child there to learn how to be a good pirate. (Or even a very BAD pirate.)

Grrr! I'm the fiercest person in the whole world!

Although Patagonia was pretty terrifying, there was one thing that made her go all silly and soppy, and that was her new little baby granddaughter. Now she sat in her office, reading a letter from her son, Marmaduke.

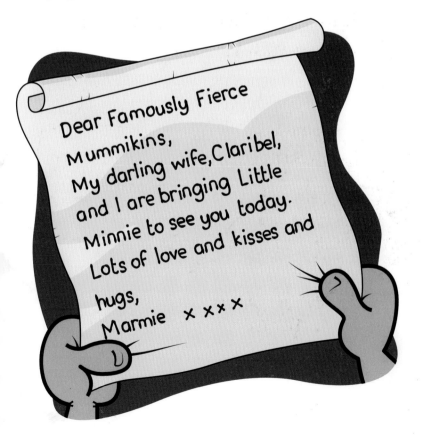

Dear Famously Fierce Mummikins,

My darling wife, Claribel, and I are bringing Little Minnie to see you today.

Lots of love and kisses and hugs,

Marmie x x x

"I'm a granny," drooled Patagonia.

She got a big ball of blue wool and began to knit a babygro for her new grandchild. What a lovely, peaceful scene.

2. An Ostrich in the Office

B ANG! The door burst open and
an ostrich hurried into the
room. It wasn't really an ostrich.

It was Miss Snitty, the school
secretary. She had long, thin legs and
an even thinner neck.

"Mrs Clatterbottom!" she
squawked. "The children are waiting
for you and …" Miss Snitty's jaw

dropped. What was Mrs Clatterbottom doing? KNITTING?

"Don't stare at me so, Snitty!" roared Patagonia, pulling off her wooden leg and chucking it at her secretary.

"Don't you dare tell anyone!"
hissed the head teacher. "I am the
fiercest head teacher in the universe!
If the children find out that I knit
woolly babygros for my little
granddaughter, they'll think I've gone
soft in the head.

"You can dive overboard and get
my leg back later," growled the head
teacher. "Let the lessons begin. Wheel
me out, Snitty!"

Patagonia Clatterbottom climbed
into her boat-pram. It had an anchor,
two sails, three flags and four
cannons. Miss Snitty wheeled the
singing head teacher out of the office.

3. Big Betty

U p on deck the new children were meeting one another. "I'm Ziggy," said a boy with a

wooden sword stuck in his belt. He
was wearing an eyepatch. He lifted
the patch and his eye fell out.

The others screamed.

"It's all right," he laughed. "It's a
joke eye. It's on a spring.

"Wow!" cried Ziggy. "Look at that
girl's hair!"

Ziggy
was
right.
Corkella's
hair was
glossy brown.
It bounced
about her head.

Corkella
grinned. "It's
never been cut,"

she told
the
others.
"Meet
Smudge and
Flo," Corkella
said to Ziggy.
Flo was a small,
slim girl. Ziggy said
that they should
call her Little
Flo.
She blushed.
Flo thought Ziggy
was wonderful.
Smudge
thought Ziggy
was a show-off and
a big-head. He was

taller than Ziggy, but a lot quieter.

Little Flo suddenly went pale. "Look!" she whispered. The pram-boat came squeaking into view.

Patagonia Clatterbottom fixed the children with a steely glare.

Little Flo felt her knees knocking together.

Smudge swallowed hard.

Corkella twisted her hair into knots.

Ziggy just glared back. He wasn't scared … yet.

"Listen to me, you horrible children. This is Pirate School, the best pirate school in the world. When I was your age, all I wanted to be when I grew up was a pirate. That little beast there – what do you want

to be when
you grow up?"

Corkella
twisted her hair
even more. "I'd
like to be a dentist."

"WHAT! This is a school for
pirates, you bird's nest! How about

you, boy? I bet you want to be a
horribly nasty pirate."

Smudge took a deep breath. "No, I
don't. I'm going to work in a fish-and-
chip shop."

"And I want to be a model,"
said Little Flo.

Patagonia Clatterbottom had another small explosion. "Listen, you're here to learn how to be pirates. You've got to be fierce and bloodthirsty, right?"

"I'd like to be a hamster," said Ziggy coolly. He really did want to be a pirate, but he also wanted to see if Mrs Clatterbottom would explode again.

She did. She beat the pram with her fists. She spluttered furiously. Her huge orange wig slipped over her face. She jabbed an angry finger at a fat cannon.

"This cannon is called Big Betty. If you children don't behave, I shall pop you inside the barrel and BOOM! The next thing you know,

you'll all be sitting on Mars!"

Smudge gulped. Corkella sneaked her hand into his and held it tightly.

"I don't believe her," she muttered under her breath, and Smudge felt a lot better.

As for Ziggy, he lifted his eyepatch again.

4. Some Pirate Lessons

The children were saved from further explosions by the arrival of Marmaduke, Claribel and Minnie.

Patagonia gurgled over the baby. Then she would suddenly glare at the children. "I'm the fiercest head teacher ever," she would hiss. "And don't you forget it!" Then she would gurgle at the baby once more. "Who's a booful liddle diddums, then?"

"You are," muttered Ziggy under his breath.

"I heard that! I shall put you in Big Betty before this day's over! Now get to your lessons at once!"

The first pirate lesson was with Mrs Muggwump, who had a rather squashed look about her. This was because she had a pet toucan which

I shall teach you how to swing on ropes.

often sat on her right shoulder. Every time the toucan turned to the left, his great big beak crashed into Mrs Muggwump's face.

After that, the children went across to Mad Maggott, who had lost one hand to a very fierce shark and now had a metal spoon instead. (The shark had also bitten his bottom, and he had a very big scar there, but he

wouldn't show it to anyone, not even his mum.)

Miss Fishgripp was small and round. She had a pink eyepatch, and she was covered in plasters. Maybe that was because she had fifteen swords stuck in her waistband.

5. What Storm?

"Time to set sail," declared the head teacher. She licked a finger and held it up to test the wind.

Corkella glanced up at the darkening sky. "It looks as if there might be a storm," she said.

"Nonsense!" bellowed Patagonia. "Just a few little clouds. All hands on deck!"

A gust of wind made all the sails rattle and flap.

"I think there might be a gale coming," suggested Smudge.

"Nonsense! Just a bit of wind. Splice the mainbrace!" Several drops of rain splattered on to the deck.

"I think it might be going to pour," said Little Flo.

"Nonsense! Just a little drizzle. Weigh anchor!"

The children hauled on the ropes. The gathering wind filled the sails, and soon the boat was heading bravely across the bay.

High above, the clouds were turning purple and black. They grew and grew until …

SPADDANGG!

Lightning slashed the sky. The wind roared and tore at the sails. Rain sliced the air and poured down upon the crew. The boat was tossed from one raging wave to another.

"We shall all be swept away!" cried Miss Snitty.

"Oh no we won't," growled Patagonia, and she tied the secretary to one of the masts.

6. Man, Woman and Baby Overboard!

The baby howled.

"We're all going to die,
Mummikins!" cried Marmaduke.

"Don't be silly. Give Minnie to me to look after."

Patagonia cuddled the baby in her boat-pram.

Another crack of lightning hit the top mast and sent it crashing into the sea.

The teachers rushed about, shouting orders.

Waylay on the grimblegrum!

"Belay the dibbleding!"

"Taggle the wobblets!"

Ziggy frowned. "What are they going on about?"

"Don't ask me," shrugged Smudge. "I think they've gone potty."

Far out at sea, a giant wave was gathering force. It rolled across the ocean, growing bigger and bigger, heaving along like some enormous monster. And then it came in sight of the little Pirate School sailing across the bay.

SHWOOOOSH!

A mountain of sea water smashed across the ship. It swept Patagonia

Clatterbottom, Little Minnie and the pram into the angry sea.

"My baby!" screamed Claribel. She raced to the edge of the boat and peered over. The pram was bobbing about on the churning water.

"Don't worry, Minnie," cried Marmaduke. "Mummy will save you!" And with that he pushed his wife overboard. "You can't do that!" shouted Corkella. "Well, I can't swim,"

Marmaduke shrugged.

Then a second wave hit him on the chest and sent him toppling overboard too.

7. Everybody to the Rescue

"Don't worry, I shall save them!" shouted Mad Maggott, diving into the sea.

A moment later, he reappeared, still shouting. "Help!" came the cry.

"I'll save him," cried Miss Fishgripp. She hurled herself into the sea too.

When she surfaced, she was wearing a surprised jellyfish on her head. She spat out a mouthful of water. "Help!" she cried.

"I'll save absolutely everyone!" cried Mrs Muggwump. She tried to jump into the sea, but her foot got caught in some rope. She ended up, dangling upside down from a mast, with her dress round her head, swinging lazily backwards and forwards in the rain.

Meanwhile, everyone else was climbing on to the pram-boat. Patagonia Clatterbottom sat, all squashed up, at the bottom, with Mad

Maggott on her lap. Claribel sat on Maggott's shoulders, and Miss Fishgripp hung on to Claribel, holding the baby. As for Marmaduke, Claribel wouldn't let him come on board at all, so he had to learn to swim after all.

8. Some Good Ideas

"**O**h dear," said Miss Snitty. "What are we to do?"
Most of the sails had been ripped

apart by the gale. The ship was half full of sea water and half full of rain water. That meant, generally speaking, that it was full up with water.

Ziggy took charge and untied Miss Snitty.

"Flo and Smudge – get some buckets and bail out the water.

Corkella, you help me get the sails down. Snitty, fetch the telescope and see if you can spot the pram."

"It's over there, floating on the waves," Miss Snitty said, pointing wildly. "But it's such a long way off. They'll topple over and drown if we don't reach them soon."

Little Flo tugged at Ziggy's arm. "Maybe we can use Big Betty," she suggested.

Ziggy glanced at the enormous

cannon. He nodded. "You're a very clever girl," he told Flo, and she blushed again. "It might just work, but it will be dangerous, and very noisy. Tie this rope round my waist," said Ziggy.

He climbed inside Big Betty's barrel. His voice sounded strange and echoey. The others could no longer see him. Even Smudge thought Ziggy was very brave. "Are you ready?" he asked.

"Yes-ess-ess-ess!" came the echo.

Corkella counted down. "Three, two, one, FIRE!"

B O O M !

Flames and smoke belched from the cannon. Big Betty almost leaped into the air. Ziggy came shooting out, with the rope trailing behind.

9. Superziggy!

O ver the water he went, whizzing through the rain and thunder and lightning.

SPLOPP-A-DOPP!

He landed right inside the pram, sending everyone else toppling into the water – all except Little Minnie. Now she lay in Ziggy's arms, fast asleep.

Patagonia Clatterbottom's wig came right off and drifted to the bottom of the ocean, where an octopus fell in love with it.

Ziggy yelled to the crew on the ship, "Haul in the rope!"

Corkella and Little Flo and Smudge all pulled on the rope. Meanwhile, the toucan tried to be very helpful. There was a loud thump as Mrs Muggwump suddenly crashed down on to the deck.

At last the children got everyone safely back on board. The rain had stopped. The wind had died away to a gentle breeze.

"Well done, Ziggy!" shouted Smudge and Little Flo and Corkella.

"What did he do?" snapped the bald head teacher.

"He saved you from the storm," Smudge pointed out. "You were washed overboard."

"Nonsense! I jumped. I did it on purpose. That was your first lesson in safety at sea."

10. Party Time

"Minnie has been saved," sighed Claribel. "I think we should celebrate."

"Good idea," agreed Patagonia.
"We shall have a pirate party. We'll
sing sea-shanties and play 'Walk the
Plank' and do all that yo-ho-ho stuff.

Shiver me timbers and wangle me riblets."

Corkella sighed. "She's gone potty again."

Little Flo nodded. "She's just a potty pirate."

Mad Maggott played the mouth-organ, Miss Snitty played the accordion, and everyone danced.

Patagonia Clatterbottom sat in a corner. She watched the fun for a while. Then she pulled out her knitting and got to work on Little Minnie's babygro.

Ziggy crept up behind her. "Are you knitting a babygro, Mrs Clatterbottom? You're not really fierce at all, are you? You're just a big softy."

Patagonia leaped to her feet. "What?! I'm the fiercest pirate in the universe. This isn't a babygro. This is

going to be my new wig – see!"

Patagonia hastily pulled the
knitting over her head.

"There! Just the job. What are you
laughing at? Stop it at once! I'll put
you all in Big Betty. Miss Snitty! How

dare you laugh at me. I'm the fiercest pirate ever. I'll make you all walk the gangplank. Ziggy – PUT YOUR EYE BACK IN AND STOP LAUGHING!"